DONKEY DIARIES

Donkey Drama

Peter Clover

ILLUSTRATED BY

Carolyn Dinan

OXFORD
UNIVERSITY PRESS

Great Clarendon Street, Oxford OX2 6DP

Oxford University Press is a department of the University of Oxford.
It furthers the University's objective of excellence in research, scholarship,
and education by publishing worldwide in

Oxford New York

Athens Auckland Bangkok Bogotá Buenos Aires
Cape Town Chennai Dar es Salaam Delhi Florence Hong Kong Istanbul
Karachi Kolkata Kuala Lumpur Madrid Melbourne Mexico City Mumbai
Nairobi Paris São Paulo Shanghai Taipei Tokyo Toronto Warsaw

Oxford is a registered trade mark of Oxford University Press
in the UK and in certain other countries

British Library Cataloguing in Publication Data available

ISBN 0-19-275124-7

3 5 7 9 10 8 6 4 2

Designed and Typeset by Mike Brain Graphic Design Limited, Oxford

Printed in Great Britain by Cox & Wyman Ltd, Reading, Berkshire

Whistlewind Farm is a fictional donkey sanctuary and the practises described, although authentic,
are not based on those used by any real donkey sanctuary.

to the loving memory of my father

All the books in this series have been read and approved
by the Folly's Farm Sanctuary for Donkeys.

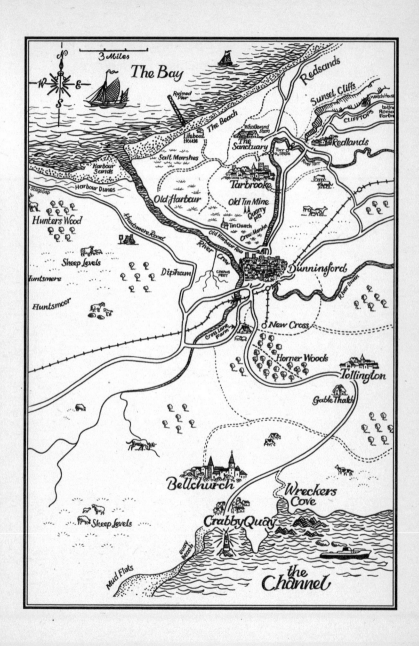

Tina was the latest resident to be enrolled at The Sanctuary. Jenny Lester liked to call the donkeys, 'residents'. It made them sound dignified and more important than just 'donkeys'.

To Jenny, Peter, and their daughter Danni, donkeys meant everything. The Sanctuary at Whistlewind Farm was the Lesters' lifelong dream—a retreat, devoted to providing a lifetime of loving care to rescued and unwanted donkeys. And each and every donkey that crossed their threshold, became an instant family member. A Sanctuary 'resident'. Tina was no exception to that rule.

Tina was a young, boisterous donkey—only six years old, with a temper that put most hooligans to shame. She was bright, lively, and totally uncontrollable. Danni loved her to bits from the first moment she saw her.

The isolation paddock—Saturday morning

Tina stood in the isolation paddock all on her own. She had been at The Sanctuary for a week, but couldn't yet be trusted to mix with the other 'residents'. She could rub noses with them across the paddock fence. And blow noisy, rasping snorts at her budding admirers. But she couldn't be trusted to behave in their company —not just yet.

Tina was fiery. She bucked and bit. She kicked and nipped. She bullied and spat. In fact, she was awful. But she was also very beautiful. Tina was the most gorgeous apricot colour you could ever possibly imagine. Apricot tinged with gold was the best way to describe her coat. With dark, chocolate-tipped ears and a dark line running the length of her back to her tufty brown tail. Yes! Tina was stunning. Probably the most beautiful donkey that Danni had ever seen.

A family from Appledere had bought Tina as company for their daughter's pony. Donkeys normally make excellent field companions. Unfortunately, in this case, Tina had terrified the poor pony to exhaustion—she had to go! It had been the same story with all her past owners. Tina had a history of hooligan behaviour. She desperately needed taking in hand, but nobody had the patience or courage to do it. Nobody, that was, up until now. Suddenly, Tina had met her match. She was nine years old and called Danni Lester.

Tina trotted a complete circuit of the enclosure, burning off steam. Her ears were perky. Her eyes were bright and alert. She saw Danni watching her.

Danni held a head collar and a lunge rein casually in her hands. Tina cleared her nostrils and blew a snuffled snort. Then she trotted over towards Danni to say, 'hello'. Despite all her faults, Tina liked company. She liked human contact and the feel of a gentle hand stroking her face and neck. But only for a short time!

Tina didn't mind the head collar, once it was wrestled on her. But she absolutely hated the lunge rein. And today, it was time for a much needed exercise in trust and control.

The lunge rein was a long rein which Danni attached to Tina's head collar. Danni held one end, at a distance, and sent the donkey trotting around her in a wide circle. She used a lungeing whip to gently tap Tina's rump and keep her moving forward. The object of the exercise was to get Tina used to being controlled. And to gradually build trust and confidence in the donkey. Tina couldn't be allowed to have her own way all the time. And she was slowly learning.

'Watch her head!' This came from Kristie, a volunteer worker at The Sanctuary. Kristie was

seventeen and bonkers about donkeys. She
ambled across to the paddock offering
encouragement.

'That's nice. Keep her moving. Keep the
whip behind her.'

Tina was going boss-eyed, looking back
across her withers, trying to see where the
gentle tickle tap-tapping on her bottom was
coming from. She kept throwing her head
round. But at least she kept moving.

'Watch her eyes,' warned Kristie. 'They're
starting to look a bit wild.'

It was true. Danni saw that Tina's expression had changed. At first, the donkey had tolerated the control and discipline of the lunging exercise. She was happy to walk, trot, and canter in neat circles. But suddenly her mood changed and she was looking for trouble. Tina was in hooligan mode!

Danni clung on tightly to the rein as the donkey bucked and kicked up her heels. Tina made no threat to Danni but threw herself into a complete strop. She circled Danni like a feisty whirlwind, snorting grumpily and braying like a drain.

'Keep that rein taut,' yelled Kristie. 'Keep her going.'

Tina was pulling hard and going like a train.

Danni dropped the whip. Suddenly she didn't feel as though she was in control any more.

'Here! Hand her over,' said a gentle voice. It was Jenny Lester. She had seen Tina playing up and came to take over.

Jenny was brilliant with donkeys. Even

nutters and hooligans. She took the rein loosely and gave it several flicks. This sudden change in the tension distracted Tina momentarily. The donkey stopped bucking and turned her head to look at Jenny.

'Whoaaahh, girl,' soothed Jenny. Her voice sounded gentle and reassuring.

Tina calmed down to a steady trot as Jenny slowly coiled the rein up in her hand.

The closer Jenny got, the slower Tina moved, until, finally, she was walking calmly at arm's length.

Jenny reached forward and stroked Tina's neck. 'Good girl! Good Tina!'

At first the donkey pulled away. Then she changed her mind and relaxed to enjoy a petting session.

'Why are you such a buzzbomb?' asked Jenny as she fondled Tina's velvet ears. 'You're nothing but a great big softy underneath that temper.' Jenny took a gingernut biscuit from her pocket and palmed the donkey a treat.

As before, Jenny noticed that half the

biscuit dropped out of Tina's mouth as she chewed. This worried Jenny.

'Go on,' she said, unclipping the rein from the head collar. 'Go and blow off some more steam before you see the tooth man.'

Jenny believed that part of Tina's bad behaviour was due to teeth problems, causing her pain. Like their hoofs, donkey's teeth grow at an alarming rate. And often develop sharp points, which cause discomfort and need regular rasping.

Tina was showing all the signs of a donkey with dental difficulties. And guess what? The vet was on his way.

Saturday afternoon—Tarbrooke

Tim Bentley was Danni's best friend. He stood waiting outside his front gate listening for the sound of galloping hoofs and whirring wheels. He didn't have to wait very long. Minutes later, Danni and her black racing donkey, Shadow, burst into view across Brooke Bridge in their painted fish-cart.

Yellow sparks flashed on the cobbles from Shadow's hoofs as he skidded to a halt, inches from Tim's feet.

'Jump in,' yelled Danni. 'We're on a mission.' Then she flicked the reins across Shadow's back, and the little donkey shot off again.

'Can we slow down a bit,' Tim laughed, hanging on for dear life. He knew it was a stupid question as soon as he'd said it. Shadow only had two speeds. Stop, and manic gallop.

'We've got to check out a "cruelty through neglect" report,' said Danni. 'Skinner's scrapyard in Redlands. Have you heard of it?'

'I don't know Redlands very well,' confessed Tim as they flew over a bump. 'But I'm sure we'll find it.'

Redlands 2.00p.m.

Redlands wasn't a very big town. But looking for the scrapyard was like searching for a needle in a haystack.

It was Shadow who eventually found it. The streets of Redlands were few and narrow. It was impossible to race around at any speed. And they didn't want to ask anyone. They were on a secret mission. Shadow was bored with walking. Suddenly he threw up his head and bellowed like a pirate. Shadow had the loudest bray in Devon—if not the universe. In fact it was more like a foghorn. It was awesome—it was ear splitting. And everyone in Redlands heard it. Including a poor little donkey hidden away in a scrapyard.

Shadow's keen ears acted like radar. They picked up a donkey's answering call and homed in on its whereabouts.

Compared to Shadow's bray, this donkey's call was no more than a pathetic wheezing. But it was enough to alert Shadow.

'He's heard something,' said Danni. She slackened the reins and gave Shadow his head. The donkey trotted off.

'There it is.' Tim pointed to a sign. Skinner's Scrapyard. 'There, behind those painted gates.'

Shadow poked his head over some panelled fencing and nuzzled nose to nose with a little silver donkey standing in a paddock next to the yard.

The silver donkey waggled its ears and hung its shaggy head over the fence, snuffling in

Danni's hand as she stroked its soft mouth.

'The poor thing's asking for food,' said Danni. She tore up a handful of grass from their side of the fence and held it out. The donkey took it, greedily.

'There's hardly anything at all growing in this paddock,' observed Tim. 'There's some grungy looking stuff along the edge here,' he said peering over the fence. 'But it's long been cropped to the root. The poor thing must be starving. Look, the rest of the paddock's just hard mud.'

Danni tore more handfuls of grass and fed the donkey great clumps of it. Then she took a proper look at the paddock and saw how horrible it was.

For a start, it was far too small. Not nearly large enough to support grazing for a fully grown donkey.

A few patches of stringy grass were managing to survive here and there, alongside a scattering of weeds. But the rest of the paddock was nothing but dry earth and mud. It was awful. But at least there was a water trough. That was one bonus.

The scrapyard next door was a mess, too. Just piles of old junk and scrap metal scattered everywhere. A wooden cart stood abandoned in a corner, covered with an old tarpaulin.

A small house was set back from the yard. Some of the window panes were cracked. One window was boarded over completely. The place looked deserted.

'Do you think the poor thing's been totally abandoned?' asked Tim.

'I don't know,' replied Danni. 'Some people live in horrible old houses like that.'

'But it's not fair to make their animals live in the same way,' said Tim. 'At least people have the choice!'

Danni agreed. The silver donkey kept nudging her hand for more food. The grass she was feeding it was green and juicy; not like the dry old grungy stuff growing sparsely in its paddock. It was such a sweet, friendly old donkey. And such a lovely colour. It must have been a pale, pewter grey once. But age had turned it almost silver. Its legs and belly were nearly white.

It looked as though a bright light was illuminating it from below.

Danni did a quick visual check so she could report details back to The Sanctuary.

14

The donkey seemed alert, although a little underweight and undernourished. Its coat was a little tatty looking but nothing a good grooming couldn't sort out. Its hoofs seemed OK—not desperate for a trim. But its eyes looked tired and heavy. That worried Danni.

She stroked its furry face and promised the donkey that they would be back. Really soon.

'Do you think we should knock and see if anyone's at home?' suggested Tim.

Danni shook her head so hard that she whipped her cheeks pink with long dark hair.

'Mum said, "observe only",' Danni reminded him. 'We're the foot soldiers. Mum's the cavalry.'

Tim laughed. He knew exactly what Danni meant.

The Sanctuary—later that afternoon

Long after the vet had gone, Tina stood peacefully, dozing in the dappled shade of a cherry tree. Tina was calm and docile. It could have been a miracle, but it wasn't. The sedative that Tim Wingfield had given her hadn't yet worn off.

'Look at Tina,' smiled Jenny. 'She's like a completely different donkey. As quiet as a lamb.'

Kristie laughed. 'But it took two attempts to give her that injection. I've never seen a donkey make such a fuss about a dental examination.'

'Tim Wingfield said it was like knocking out an elephant. But it was the only way that Tina would allow the vet to examine inside her mouth.'

But Jenny was right about Tina's teeth. They were in a terrible condition and causing her a great deal of pain. Her treatment was starting tomorrow.

The other visitor

It was just after four o'clock when a second visitor dropped in to The Sanctuary. This visitor was from a local theatre company. He was an actor and looking for a donkey to star in their forthcoming production of *The Further Adventures of Don Quixote*.

'We can't afford the animal actors' agency fees,' he said, 'but we can pay £200, from our production budget. It's only for a one night's limited performance, so it's a good offer.' The actor told Jenny that Westair TV, the local West Country television station, was going to broadcast the performance, live on Channel 4.

£200 was a lot of money. But Jenny wasn't keen to let any of The Sanctuary residents perform in a TV special.

'£200 would buy a lot of barley straw,' whispered Kristie.

'And there's the vet's bills to think of,' added Peter. 'Tina's teeth are going to bite into our medical allowance.' He grinned at the pun. '£200 would really help out!'

It was true. Jenny knew only too well that £200 would help The Sanctuary finances. It was one offer they couldn't really afford to turn away.

'What exactly would be involved?' Jenny asked, casually, trying not to sound too interested.

The actor explained details of the performance. They required a donkey to be on the stage set for a duration of one and a half hours. For most of the performance, the donkey would be standing in view, on the sidelines. But for the last fifteen minutes, in the final act, the donkey would be in the spotlight, centre stage. And be required to carry a small child across the auditorium.

There would be one run through. One dress rehearsal. And one performance. In total, it added up to four and a half hours' work.

Jenny said she would think about it. The actor said he would like to look at some of the donkeys while he was there. Then he saw Tina.

'That's the one,' he exclaimed. 'That's the donkey I want for the play.'

He was very impressed with Tina's colouring.

'She will look fantastic under the spotlights,' he said. 'I have never seen such a beautiful donkey. She's almost golden! And so serene! The TV cameras will love her.'

Tina opened one brown, lazy eye. Blinked her long lashes. Then went back to dozing peacefully in the cool shade. The sedative was still working its magic.

'I'm not sure about Tina's suitability,' said Jenny. 'She's quite new here, and has a bit of a fiery temperament. Maybe one of the other residents would be more suitable.'

But, no! The actor wanted Tina. 'She will be perfect,' he said. 'I will call back again on Wednesday afternoon. That will give you a few days to think about it.' Then he left.

Sunday morning

The vet didn't normally come out on Sundays, except for emergencies. But Tim Wingfield was a great friend of The Sanctuary, and wanted to begin Tina's treatment as soon as possible. The

donkey's teeth needed rasping, urgently. Tim wanted to start very gently at first to get Tina used to the sound and feel of the rasp. Usually, once the rasping gets going, the donkeys seem to enjoy the sensation. They seem to understand that the sharp points on their teeth, which have been causing them pain, are being dealt with. Some donkeys need a little sedation at first, until they get used to the process. Tina was no exception.

The first rasping was over in ten minutes. But on examination, Tim had discovered that two of Tina's back teeth needed to be completely removed. They were loose and crumbled under treatment. They must have been causing Tina pain when she ate. So out they came.

Poor Tina was so zonked out with the sedative that she didn't know what was happening.

After the vet had gone, she stood in a daze with her fuzzy chin resting on the top bar of the paddock fence. That was exactly how the actor found her when he came to The Sanctuary for an unexpected visit.

The actor's name was Stephen Gregory. This time he had brought his little boy along to see the donkeys. His son, Toby, was seven years old and had learning difficulties.

When Toby saw all the donkeys, his eyes grew wide, to the size of headlamps. And his face lit up like a Christmas tree. His father had never seen Toby so interested in anything before.

Skinner's yard—Redlands—midday

Danni kicked in the brake wedges under the wheels of Shadow's fish-cart and grabbed the sack of feed.

'Come on, Tim,' she urged. 'Let's give the old donkey a feast.'

Jenny had intended to come along to the yard, too. She had planned to call on Mr Skinner and question him about his donkey. But at the last minute she decided to stay with Tina while the vet rasped her teeth. She sent

Danni and Tim instead, with a sackful of fodder. She could visit Mr Skinner at a later date.

'Don't do anything except feed the donkey,' warned Jenny. 'I don't want you to get involved with Mr Skinner.'

Danni remembered what her mum had said as she leaned over the panelled fence and held out a clump of sweet barley straw.

At first the little silver donkey took no notice of them. Then Danni called to him and very, very slowly he raised his head and looked across the paddock. His ears tick-tocked back and forth.

'Come on, boy. Come and get it. This is proper food, better than old bits of grungy grass.' Danni waved the sweet smelling straw.

Then the donkey's nose twitched. He snuffled a wheezy snort and began, very slowly, to pick his way towards them on wobbly legs. He seemed very weak and almost stumbled once. But he kept going.

'Come on, boy,' encouraged Danni—and at last he managed to reach them.

Danni hand-fed the straw to the little donkey. He munched happily, and asked for more.

Tim scrambled over the fence and dropped into the paddock. He'd noticed there was an outside tap above the drinking trough, and refreshed the water.

The donkey seemed a little alarmed at first as Tim landed next to him. He flicked back his ears and rolled his eyes. It was then that Danni first noticed that something was wrong. The donkey's eyes seemed dull and lifeless.

Danni reached across the fence and calmed the donkey with her touch. Then she fed him some chopped carrots and apples from a bag and tried to look closely at his eyes. She waved

her free hand in front of the donkey's face. The donkey didn't flinch. The donkey didn't even see her hand. The poor little thing was blind.

The Sanctuary—Sunday afternoon

When Danni and Shadow arrived back at The Sanctuary, after dropping Tim off, Stephen Gregory and Toby were just leaving. They had just spent two enjoyable hours with The Sanctuary donkeys. Normally, Toby would have thrown six screaming tantrums in that time. He wasn't really a naughty boy—he simply had a problem. He couldn't help his bad behaviour. Finding things that interested Toby was difficult. Toby had never seen donkeys before and he was totally fascinated by these gentle, docile creatures.

Toby couldn't believe it when he saw Shadow pulling the fish-cart up the drive. He became so excited, he wouldn't get into his father's car until he could have a ride.

Danni and Shadow took Toby for a quick spin around the yard. And Toby was as good as gold.

'He's never gone this long without a tantrum before,' marvelled Stephen Gregory. 'He's not deliberately difficult, he just has a difficult problem.' The actor couldn't thank Jenny enough.

'Don't forget about the donkey for our play,' he said, gently reminding Jenny about Tina. 'All the profits are going towards a charity for children with learning difficulties. I'll call by on Wednesday for your answer. Fingers crossed.'

'Fingers crossed,' copied Toby. Apparently he hardly ever spoke.

Jenny and Danni smiled as the actor and his son drove away. Little Toby had given Jenny an idea.

The Sanctuary Kitchen

Danni told her parents all about the little donkey in Skinner's Yard. 'He's blind,' explained Danni.

'I'm certain of it. We left him plenty of food and gave him fresh water, but he just stands there staring straight ahead. It must be awful for him living like that,' she continued. Danni was on her soapbox now. 'He hasn't got a proper paddock. And he desperately needs company. It's criminal that this Skinner man can treat his donkey like this!'

Jenny told Danni to calm down.

'I'll go and check it out myself tomorrow,' she said. 'You did a good job, Danni. Excellent observation.'

Danni grinned and twirled a piece of her long dark hair around a finger. She liked it when Jenny praised her for doing a good surveillance job. It made her feel like a New York cop. Danni Lester—NYPD.

'Now, if you want to earn extra brownie points,' added Jenny. 'How about giving Tina a gentle grooming while she's still dozy from the sedative? Get her used to as much hands-on contact as possible.'

Danni saluted. 'Consider it done!'

27

Tarbrooke—Monday

Danni decided to go home from school the long way round—via Redlands. Tim said he'd come along too, even though he only lived down the lane from Tarbrooke Middle School. Home via Redlands for Tim was the extra long way round. But Redlands meant Skinner's yard and the poor little blind donkey.

Danni and Tim rode their bikes along the country lane. Danni had a plastic bag stuffed with barley straw and a few carrots in her pocket. Tim had saved an apple from his lunchbox. Skinner's donkey was in for a feast.

They stashed their bikes against the panelled fencing and leaned over into the barren paddock next to the yard.

They quickly looked around, but there was no sign of the little blind donkey.

Danni tried calling and clicking with her tongue hoping that it would appear by magic. But there was nowhere for it to hide.

Tim whistled in vain. They both waved the barley straw. But there was no donkey.

'Maybe he's already been taken to The Sanctuary,' suggested Tim. Danni brightened. Maybe her mum had already been to collect him. She hadn't thought of that!

Another quick check just to make sure. Then they were off, mega pedal.

The Sanctuary—Whistlewind Farm

Tim rode with Danni all the way back to Whistlewind Farm. By this time, they were both convinced that the little silver donkey had been rescued by Jenny Lester and imagined it settling into a safe paddock. They were very disappointed when they found out that they were wrong.

'The donkey wasn't there,' explained Jenny. 'I found Skinner's yard, but no donkey! The paddock was empty when I arrived.'

Danni's mouth hung open in disbelief.

'What could have happened to him?' she asked. 'He's blind. He couldn't possibly go anywhere on his own.'

'Perhaps he's been taken away by someone else,' said Tim.

'By who?' questioned Danni. 'And why?'

'I suppose Mr Skinner is the obvious choice,' said Jenny. 'I knocked at the house but there was no answer. He wasn't out working because I noticed that the donkey cart was still in the yard. I'm afraid there's not much we can do if we don't know where Mr Skinner or the old donkey are!'

It really bothered Danni. She could think of nothing else all evening. Or the following morning. Fragments of a plan began to form in her mind. She was determined to find that donkey. She decided to tell Tim about it at school, during morning break.

Tarbrooke Middle School—Tuesday morning

Danni approached Tim in the playground with a rucksack full of Sanctuary flyers.

'I've brought these,' she explained. 'I thought we could deliver them, after school, around Redlands, and use them as an excuse to knock on doors.'

'Brilliant,' said Tim. 'Maybe someone knows where Mr Skinner and his donkey have gone.' Tim thought for a moment, then added, 'What if we find out that they've moved away and left the scrapyard to live somewhere else?'

'I hope not,' replied Danni. 'We'll never be able to rescue the poor donkey, then!'

The day seemed to drag. By the time the home bell rang, Danni and Tim were raring to go.

They threw themselves onto their bikes and pedalled furiously out of the school gates. Redlands was a good twenty minutes ride away so they put their heads down and went for full pedal power.

Redlands

Skinner's yard was not only empty, it seemed totally and utterly deserted. The house held an eerie silence as Danni and Tim approached the front door. They thought they would check the house again, just in case Mr Skinner was there.

Jenny would go mad if she knew what they were up to.

They rang the doorbell and listened as a hollow buzz echoed inside the empty shell of a hallway. Then nothing! No footfalls. No one yelling 'go away' through the letterbox. Not a sound. No squeaky floorboards. Nothing! Except silence.

'Well, it was worth a try,' consoled Tim.

'Come on, let's go.' Danni shivered. 'This place gives me the creeps.'

The flyer drop from house to house wasn't very successful either. None of the people they spoke to knew very much about Mr Skinner. Or what had happened to him. They knew he had a donkey, but they never said anything bad about the way he treated it. In fact most people seemed to think that Mr Skinner was very fond of Samson—that was the donkey's name.

However, most of the people they spoke to did say that they hadn't seen Mr Skinner and Samson out collecting scrap metal for quite some time. Possibly months.

The woman who ran the corner shop, said she thought that Mr Skinner had been ill. But she couldn't say for sure. It was only when Danni and Tim were ready to leave Redlands that someone approached them with all the information they were looking for.

The Sanctuary—Whistlewind Farm

Kristie was in the isolation paddock with Tina. They were lungeing. Kristie held the long rein while Tina pranced around her in circles like a circus pony.

The change in Tina, since her dental treatment, was astounding. She was still a hooligan, at times. But a loveable, reformed hooligan.

Tina was much calmer, and friendlier towards her handlers now that her teeth were being sorted out. The vet was coming to give Tina her final rasping the following morning. And the good news was that she now only needed a small amount of sedative before treatment. Tina seemed to understand that the gentle filing of her teeth was helping her.

Kristie touched Tina with the lunge whip and took her into a rolling canter. The boisterous donkey was loving every minute of it. Kristie smiled and clicked her tongue. 'Good girl, Tina. Good girl. Keep going.'

The other Sanctuary residents came up to the fence to watch. Tina enjoyed all the attention. She was really showing off.

Finally, Kristie reeled Tina in and gave her a moment of cuddles. The donkey closed her eyes and licked the hand which fondled her soft velvet muzzle.

Then, after a few minutes, the hugging turned into a wrestling match as Kristie tried to unfasten Tina's head collar. Hooligans rule, OK!

The other donkeys started laughing. Well, it seemed like laughing. Heads were thrown back, ears waggled, and teeth grinned as they hee-haawed and brayed at the top of their lungs.

The commotion made Tina stop. Kristie took advantage of the sudden time out and whipped off the head collar. Tina looked embarrassed. She turned her back on the other 'residents' and walked to the other side of the paddock, sulking.

Back in Redlands

Danni and Tim were just about to leave Redlands when a young voice called out to them.

Danni nearly fell off her bike as she spun round to see who was calling.

'Are you looking for Samson?' enquired a young girl who suddenly scrambled over a garden wall. 'I saw you the other day feeding Skinner's donkey,' she added.

The girl was about the same age as Danni and Tim. She was as thin as a reed and wore a black and yellow striped jumper. Tim thought she looked like a wasp. Her name was Melody.

'He's been taken away by Pettigrew,' Melody continued, without waiting for an answer. 'Old Skinner's been ill for months and now he's in Dunninsford hospital. My dad drove him there in the ambulance.' Melody stopped to catch her breath. 'It was me who phoned The Sanctuary and told them about Samson. He's not being looked after properly. And now Pettigrew's got him.'

'Who's Pettigrew?' asked Danni and Tim in unison.

'He's horrible,' sneered Melody. 'He lives in the Watch House up on Sunset Cliffs. He grows vegetables in his market garden and sells them on a stall in Dunninsford.'

'But why has he taken Samson?' asked Tim.

'I think Skinner owed Pettigrew money. So he's taken the donkey instead to make it work for him.'

'Does Mr Skinner know about this?' asked Danni. Melody didn't know. But Danni and Tim were determined to find out.

The Sanctuary—Wednesday morning

After the vet's visit, Jenny had planned to drive into Dunninsford and visit Mr Skinner in hospital. Danni's report from Redlands was enough to convince Jenny that there was a donkey out there, in need of The Sanctuary's help.

The thought of a little blind donkey being taken away from its home and put to work for a complete stranger, made Jenny's blood boil. She was anxious to get to the bottom of this.

But first, the vet.

Tina was in a bit of a grumpy mood when Tim Wingfield arrived. Fortunately, the vet was getting used to Tina's tantrums.

This was the last rasping to complete Tina's treatment. Tim had expected her to be used to the handling and filing by now. But Tina was being really stroppy, so he had to tranquillize her to calm her down. Tina stood with her head hung low, snoozing on her feet. It was much easier when Tina was knocked out like this.

The vet took advantage of the dozing donkey and gave her a thorough examination. Tina was in perfect health. In fact, she was in perfect condition, too. Her apricot coloured coat shone like gold in the morning sunlight. She looked absolutely beautiful.

Jenny and Peter were looking at the vet's bill when Stephen Gregory turned up with Toby. The little boy looked ready to burst with excitement. He was all bright eyes and smiles.

'Donkey, donkey, donkey,' he sang; over and over.

'Sorry, I'm early,' apologized the actor. 'I couldn't keep Toby away.' He told Jenny how the donkeys at The Sanctuary had changed

Toby's life, almost overnight. 'Since our last visit Toby's behaviour has improved so much,' he said. 'All Toby talks about is when can he come and see the donkeys again. It's the first time he's ever been interested in anything enough to talk about it. It's brilliant.'

Jenny looked at Peter and smiled.

'That's donkeys working their magic,' she said, then told the actor that he could stay as long as Toby liked.

Stephen Gregory asked if The Sanctuary had thought any more about renting Tina to the theatre company.

Peter folded the vet's bill in half and raised an eyebrow at Jenny. They didn't have much choice. There were bills to pay—and they had a donkey for hire!

Jenny's main concern was that Tina would behave herself. Looking at her now, sedated and dozing in the sunshine, butter wouldn't melt in her mouth.

Jenny decided to work with Tina personally every day. The play was two weeks away. Jenny could work miracles in two weeks! She told the actor that Tina would be delighted to star in their production. Then she set off for Dunninsford, wondering if she had done the right thing.

The Watch House—Sunset Cliffs

Danni and Tim were planning to do a bit of spying. After school, they left Tarbrooke, and headed towards The Sanctuary. They crossed the broad, shallow river at Tarr Steps. It was a great shortcut to Sunset Cliffs.

Danni and Tim sat on their bikes, overlooking the cliff top. The beach below and the sea beyond stretched away as far as they could see. The Watch House stood on guard. Dark and silent.

'It looks spooky,' whispered Danni.

'It's weird,' agreed Tim.

The stone house sat right on the edge of the cliff top. It almost looked as if it was about to fall off, and tumble down into the sea.

The land surrounding the house was a 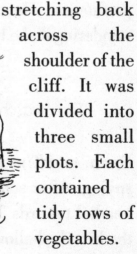 market garden, stretching back across the shoulder of the cliff. It was divided into three small plots. Each contained tidy rows of vegetables.

There was

a small shed in one of the plots. And a greenhouse which leaned against the house. An abandoned heap of rusty, ancient farm machinery lay against a stinking compost heap. But there was no sign of Samson the donkey.

'Do you think Melody could have made a mistake?' queried Tim. 'There's no sign of a donkey anywhere!'

'She seemed quite certain,' Danni reminded him. 'She knew all about Pettigrew, didn't she? And why would she make something up like that?'

'But where's Samson?' exclaimed Tim.

They talked about creeping up to the house and peering through the windows. But Danni knew that her mum would go mental if they got caught.

'Observe and report,' that was Danni's motto.

'Maybe Pettigrew's already got Samson out working at a market,' said Tim.

Danni felt awful. She couldn't just leave without knowing what had happened to the little blind donkey. Then she had a sudden thought.

'He could be locked up in that shed!'

Tim looked horrified.

'You wait here,' said Danni. 'I'm going to check it out.'

It wasn't worth Tim even thinking of trying to stop her. So he didn't bother. He just kept quiet and watched her slip across the meadow grass to the wooden shed behind the Watch House.

At any minute, he expected Pettigrew to come charging out of the house. But he didn't. Danni reached the shed and tried the door. It was locked.

There was no window so she couldn't check inside.

'Samson!' Danni whispered the donkey's name through a gap in the door. She strained her ears to listen, and thought she heard a muffled wheeze coming from inside. She couldn't be certain.

Danni wanted to break the door down, but she knew *that* was impossible. And wrong. Instead, she slinked back to her bike, and chased Tim home to The Sanctuary.

Dunninsford

Jenny was feeling really pleased with herself. The trip to Dunninsford hospital had been a great success. Mr Skinner was easy to find. He was the grumpy old man in Wellington Ward. All the nurses knew Mr Skinner. He hadn't stopped moaning since he was brought in.

But Mr Skinner was very sick. He was going to be in hospital for a long time. The old man was very upset when Jenny started talking about Samson. It turned out that he was really genuinely fond of the little blind donkey.

'I've not been able to look after him properly for months,' confessed Mr Skinner, sadly. 'But I would never want anything bad to happen to him. We've been together for years.'

Jenny asked Mr Skinner about Pettigrew. Suddenly, the old man looked frightened. He wouldn't say anything against him, but Jenny guessed that this Pettigrew wasn't a very nice man.

'He's got my donkey,' said Mr Skinner. 'I

never said he could take Samson. But I owe him money and there's nothing I can do.'

Jenny told him there was plenty that he could do.

'Write me a letter,' she explained, 'saying that you'd like us to look after Samson for you at The Sanctuary. And I promise you that we'll take care of everything until you come out of here.'

At first, Mr Skinner didn't understand. But after Jenny told him all about Whistlewind Farm, he couldn't wait to write the letter.

The Sanctuary would take care of Samson for as long as it was necessary.

The Sanctuary—Whistlewind Farm

Danni and Jenny arrived back at The Sanctuary at the same time. Immediately they were surrounded by braying donkeys, pushing and nosing their way close for fussing and a possible treat. Gingernuts and peppermints were a high priority.

Jenny broke up some biscuits and popped pieces into as many pouting mouths as she could manage. Danni tickled hairy ears and scratched bristly chins as she handed out Polos. It was always great coming home to The Sanctuary.

Teatime—The Sanctuary Kitchen

'So you've got a letter from this Mr Skinner?' asked Peter Lester, twirling a fork into the pile of spaghetti on his plate.

Jenny waved the envelope and grinned.

'I'll take the horsebox up to the Watch House first thing tomorrow,' she said, 'and collect Samson.'

'Do you think Pettigrew will just hand the donkey over without an argument?' Peter was concerned.

Jenny raised her 'no-nonsense' eyebrow. 'Oh, I thought I'd take Martin Green along for the ride,' she said. 'The sight of an RSPCA inspector in uniform is always good insurance.'

Peter knew there was no reason to be too worried about Pettigrew. Jenny's determination could prove very persuasive when she was rescuing a donkey.

'I think Pettigrew's keeping Samson locked up,' announced Danni between mouthfuls of pasta. She confessed and told her parents about the funny noises she heard coming from inside his shed.

Jenny wasn't too pleased to hear that Danni and Tim had been snooping out at the Watch House. But she was glad of the tip-off. Locking up a donkey was abominable.

'If you go really early,' pleaded Danni, 'then I could come with you, before school.'

'It's not an outing,' remarked Jenny flatly. 'It's serious Sanctuary business.'

'I won't get in the way,' promised Danni. 'I'll stay in the horsebox and . . .'

'No,' said Jenny firmly. The eyebrow went up.

Danni tried one last time.

'But Samson knows me. He'll remember me feeding him in the yard. Being blind, he's going to be really scared with loads of strangers around.'

That was true. Jenny realized that Samson would probably indeed be very distressed when they collected him. A friendly, familiar voice would be a great asset. Jenny relented.

'OK,' she smiled faintly. 'But you stay in the cab, and keep out of sight when we talk with Pettigrew.'

'Thanks, Mum!'

Thursday—the Watch House—Sunset Cliffs

It was seven thirty when The Sanctuary horsebox passed through Redlands and took the road to Sunset Cliffs.

Danni sat up front between Martin Green and Jenny in the horsebox cab. She put her feet up on the dashboard and hugged her knees as she stared through the windscreen. Up ahead, the Watch House loomed, like a dark shadow on the horizon. A shiver ran along the length of her spine.

Dark, ragged clouds skidded across the sky. It looked like rain was coming.

'There it is,' pointed Danni.

The Watch House was tall and thin. And black. Over the years, the wind and salt from the sea had weathered the stone and brickwork to a burnt charcoal grey. Today, with no sun upon its roof, the Watch House looked as black as soot.

There was an overgrown lawn, which sloped away from the house to the edge of the cliff top.

But there was still no sign of any donkey.

'There's the shed.' Danni pointed again. Her finger jabbed at the air in the direction of a small, wooden potting shed in one of the vegetable plots.

'It's barely big enough to keep a rabbit in, let alone a donkey,' exclaimed Jenny. Her face burned red with anger.

The horsebox pulled up short of the house. They parked next to a wooden sign warning the public of the crumbling cliff top. It advised visitors to keep well away from the edge.

'You stay here,' ordered Jenny, 'until we've got the donkey.' Then she jumped out of the cab and marched with Martin Green up to the front of the house.

The idea was to call early and catch Pettigrew by surprise. The letter of guardianship from Mr Skinner was safely tucked away in Jenny's jacket pocket.

Pettigrew turned out to be an early riser. No sooner had Jenny rung the bell than the door flew open. Pettigrew had already seen them coming. He didn't like visitors. He made that quite clear.

Jenny explained to Pettigrew why they were there. She showed him Mr Skinner's letter.

'This document gives us temporary legal ownership of the donkey,' announced Jenny.

Pettigrew shrugged. 'I don't know what you're talking about,' he lied. 'There's no donkey here. Skinner must be losing his marbles.'

Jenny and Martin Green exchanged worried glances.

'I have the authority to search this property,' bluffed Martin.

'Go ahead,' leered Pettigrew. 'You won't find anything!' Then he slammed the door shut.

Jenny was so angry. She wanted to batter the front door down, but knew of course that she couldn't.

'Let's check out that shed,' suggested Jenny.

Martin was already on the case.

It came as no surprise to find that the shed was locked with a big rusty padlock. Jenny looked back at the house and saw the net curtains twitch. Pettigrew was obviously spying on them.

Jenny put her ear to the door and listened carefully. Not a sound. She spoke through a crack in the wood and made snuffling, donkey noises. But the shed remained silent.

'We could try asking him to unlock it,' suggested Jenny.

'Not much chance of that,' replied Martin.

'And we really need a proper search warrant to force a legal entry.'

'Could we risk it and heave the door in?' asked Jenny. Martin's disapproving look told her they couldn't.

'Then we've no alternative but to go away and get that search warrant.'

Danni had been straining her eyes in the horsebox cab, trying to see what was going on at the house. She decided to sneak out and creep up closer for a better view. She picked her way secretly through one of the vegetable plots and was hiding behind a screen, thick with runner beans, when she heard Martin Green and her mum talking.

Danni couldn't believe it. They'd come this far and now they were being forced to return empty handed, simply because rotten old Pettigrew wouldn't unlock his shed.

By the time they come back with a search warrant, thought Danni, Pettigrew will have hidden Samson somewhere miles away and they'll never find him. It was too much to bear.

As Jenny and Martin walked away Danni stepped out from her hiding place. In her hand she held a big flat stone. Danni knew she would be in mega trouble over what she was about to do. But she couldn't help herself. There was a donkey's welfare at stake. And Danni wasn't about to let Pettigrew make fools of them. She took a deep breath and marched quickly up to the shed.

Then, three things happened, all at the same time. Jenny turned around. Pettigrew flew out of his back door. And Danni smashed the shed's padlock.

The Sanctuary—Whistlewind Farm

Peter Lester glanced at his watch and wondered how things were going with the rescue mission at Sunset Cliffs. It was eight o'clock.

'Penny for your thoughts,' called Kristie from across the yard as she swept out a stable in preparation for the expected newcomer. Her fizzy mane of strawberry blonde hair billowed out behind her like a cloud as she worked.

'They should be on their way back by now,' smiled Peter, hopefully. But suddenly he remembered an old saying his Granny Lester used to quote: 'Never count your chickens before they're hatched.' And he started to worry.

The Watch House

'Oi! Get away from there!' Pettigrew was yelling at the top of his lungs, and racing down the path.

Danni pulled the shed door open and a little silver donkey shot out like a bullet.

Danni jumped to one side, out of the way, as Samson thundered past.

Jenny lunged forward and tried to grab the donkey's head collar. But Samson was obviously terrified and thundered blindly past in a mad gallop.

Pettigrew's yelling didn't help either. It drove

Samson to the very edge of the cliff top, where miraculously, the little donkey stopped.

Martin Green grabbed at Pettigrew to stop him approaching Samson and possibly sending the donkey hurtling off the edge.

'You're in a lot of trouble,' threatened Martin. Pettigrew shrugged him off and sneered.

'Just take the stupid donkey and get off my property!' he snapped. 'It's as blind as a bat and no use to anyone, anyway.' Then he skulked back to the house without looking back.

Samson stood dangerously right on the very shoulder of the cliff top. His hoofs were no more than half a metre from the edge and a sheer drop to the beach below.

Danni froze. Her mouth dropped open like the 'o' in horror. She stared at the little donkey tottering on the brink of disaster. Willing him not to step forward. She felt awful. This was all her fault.

Waves rolled and crashed on the beach below. Gulls soared and screamed overhead. They seemed to be calling, 'Get back. Get back!'

And the little donkey trembled from head to foot. His long, bristly ears waggled frantically, listening to all the strange sounds around him. He seemed to sense that he was only inches from a sheer drop. Samson cocked his head, listening to the surf below.

Danni desperately wanted to do something to help. Jenny and Martin came and stood by her side.

'I'm sorry, Mum,' sighed Danni, faintly. 'This is all my fault.'

'Hushh!' whispered Jenny. She placed a hand on Danni's shoulder. 'No one could have known that this would happen.'

Jenny made a move to step forward. Samson's nostrils twitched as he caught her unfamiliar scent. The blind donkey gave a pathetic whicker and backed away. His rear hoofs were so close to the edge. Danni felt sick.

Loose stones fell away from the turf as the cliff top suddenly began to crumble away beneath the donkey's weight.

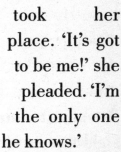

'He's going to fall,' panicked Danni. She pulled her mum back and took her place. 'It's got to be me!' she pleaded. 'I'm the only one he knows.'

Danni edged her way forward as slowly and carefully as she

dared. She stretched out her hand and gently whispered the donkey's name. 'Here, Samson. I'm coming, boy. Here, Samson. Good boy.'

Samson's ears flicked forward as he recognized a friendly voice. He lifted his head and sniffed the air. Then he wheezed a greeting. 'Eee yawwww!'

Danni's voice seemed to soothe the little blind donkey. She kept talking as she slowly closed the gap between them.

Samson seemed to be waiting for her. But as Danni reached forward and grabbed his head collar, the cliff top beneath him crumbled away.

The Sanctuary

Peter Lester checked his watch again. It was eight fifteen. He toyed with the idea of ringing Jenny on her mobile, but decided against it. He leaned on the paddock fence and Tina wandered up for a nuzzle.

Peter spoke to the donkey. She listened

carefully with her ears angled at 90 degrees from the side of her head. 'I'll give them five more minutes, then I'll phone!' he said.

Tina was feeling mischievous. She lunged forward and snatched the mobile from Peter's grasp then galloped across the pasture with it clamped between her freshly rasped teeth. Wrestling with a hooligan to get the phone back at least took Peter's mind off things.

The Clifftops—Sunset Cliffs

Jenny gasped as Samson's hind legs seemed to sink down along with the crumbling cliff top. Danni had a firm hold of the head collar and could have easily been dragged down with him.

But the little blind donkey had lightning reflexes. The moment he felt the earth move, he kicked out with all his strength.

His amazing effort sent him scrabbling with a frantic bound to the safety of solid ground.

Danni threw her arms around Samson's neck

and hugged him tightly. She wasn't sure who was shaking the most. The donkey or herself.

The Sanctuary—Saturday morning

Tina was in the isolation paddock. Only now she wasn't on her own. Samson was sharing the paddock with her. This arrangement was only intended to be on a trial basis. But something incredible happened the moment the two 'residents' were introduced. Tina transformed herself from a hooligan into a baby lamb. Not literally. She didn't turn white and woolly or anything like that. She just became gentle, docile—and nice!

Even when Danni took Tina through her lungeing paces, the reformed hooligan behaved perfectly.

'Perhaps it's the after effects of the tranquillizers she's been given for her teeth,' joked Peter.

But it wasn't. It was Samson. The little blind donkey had an amazing calming effect on our Tina. They blew air up each other's nostrils the

first second they met. They nuzzled and groomed each other as though they had been friends for life.

Both donkeys were obviously desperate for the right company. And they found it in each other at The Sanctuary.

That afternoon, Stephen Gregory and Toby came for a visit. The actor was even more impressed with Tina than ever before. He wanted to take some publicity photographs to promote the forthcoming play.

Tina posed perfectly, while the actor clicked away with his camera, capturing the donkey's beauty, poise, and charm on film.

Toby discovered Samson with wide eyes. The little boy was mesmerized by the docile silver donkey. He pressed his face close against Samson's woolly neck. Toby understood that Samson was blind, and this made the little donkey even more special to him. Samson seemed to have the same calming effect on Toby as he had on Tina.

When it was time to leave there were no tantrums, no screaming. And no tears. There had been a little donkey magic at work.

The Roman fortress—one week later

Danni and Tim biked it to the fortress straight from school. The first stage rehearsal was taking place at four thirty. Jenny was bringing Tina from The Sanctuary in the horsebox.

Danni was surprised to find that Jenny and Tina hadn't arrived yet.

The Further Adventures of Don Quixote was being staged outdoors, in the Roman fortress, against a backdrop of ancient ruins and distant, sparkling sea. The one and only performance was to take place in the evening. The last scene would have the fading sunset as its final curtain. The production promised to be a televised masterpiece. Everyone was very excited.

Tim nudged Danni in the ribs.

'Here they come.'

The Sanctuary horsebox trundled into view and parked itself against a Corinthian column.

A huddle of actors, including Stephen Gregory, turned to watch as Jenny opened the rear doors, lowered the ramp, and led out not one, but two donkeys.

A short, dumpy, balding man—who turned out to be the director—waddled over, flapping his arms, sighing heavily.

Danni thought he looked like a duck.

'At last! At last,' exclaimed Mr Coot. 'I was beginning to think we had lost one of our star members.'

Tina eyed Mr Coot, the director, suspiciously.

Please don't play up again, thought Jenny to herself. Please!

The reason that she was late in the first place was because Tina wouldn't get into the horsebox without Samson.

Over the last week, Tina had become inseparable from the little blind donkey. She had flatly refused to clamber aboard without her new friend.

'Why have you brought two donkeys?' asked Mr Coot. 'Our budget can only afford *one* donkey. And there is only a part for *one* donkey.'

Mr Coot had no knowledge of Tina's history. And Jenny didn't want to upset the apple cart by telling him that Tina wouldn't behave without Samson. Instead she smiled and said, 'He's Tina's agent. You know what stars are like? Won't go anywhere without an agent!'

Mr Coot thought this was funny. Really funny. His laugh came in short bursts. It sounded more like quacking, noted Jenny.

The stage rehearsal went brilliantly. It was a great success. Tina's role wasn't terribly demanding. Most of the time she just had to stand off centre stage, looking professional.

There was quite a lot of action going on around her though. Tina's ears tick-tocked and twitched all over the place, as the actors delivered their lines and went through their paces. But she behaved extremely well, and kept a constant check on Samson's whereabouts. The little blind donkey snoozed on his feet under the canvas shade of the refreshment trailer. He woke now and then, to sample the tasty titbits passed to him by the catering assistant. Her name was Lynne Gregory.

'This is Samson, isn't it?' she asked Jenny. 'My son, Toby, talks about nothing else these days. I can't thank you enough for introducing him to the donkeys at The Sanctuary.'

Lynne told Jenny how difficult it was to get some children with learning difficulties to show an interest in things. How difficult it was to get Toby to communicate. And how pleased she was that her son had found something he really enjoyed. Something his special needs teachers could use, to work on with him.

Lynne Gregory asked Jenny if she could bring a group of children from Toby's class to visit the donkeys at The Sanctuary. Jenny thought it was an excellent idea. She had already been thinking about starting special visiting days for children with learning difficulties. Toby had given her the idea. It was just one more way to use that special donkey magic.

Friday—one week later

The entire acting and production cast were gathered at the Roman fortress on the headland of Sunset Cliffs. Danni was giving Tina last minute grooming. She wasn't sure whose nerves she was trying to calm. Tina's, or her own. It was so exciting!

They were about to run through a full dress rehearsal of the play. At the last minute, Danni had been given a part. She was to play the role of a page to Don Quixote. She didn't have to act or speak any lines. She just had to lead Tina on and off stage as the play progressed. And in the last scene, hold a small child safely on Tina's back as the donkey crossed the full width of the stage against the setting sun.

The previous page was a little scared of Tina. The boy was nervy and jumped each time Tina smiled and showed her new teeth.

Mr Coot thought it would be best if Tina was handled by someone she knew and trusted. It was just as well—Tina wasn't too sure about the dazzling costumes or the sudden appearance of spears, shields, and swords. And when the actors began to deliver their lines in booming voices, to be heard in every corner of the ruins, it was all Danni could do to keep Tina under control. Nobody seemed to notice, but Danni mentioned it to her mum.

'I think she's got stage fright,' worried Danni. 'All that shouting and brandishing of swords. Tina thinks she's being attacked!'

But it was worse than that. Much worse. Tina actually thought that Samson was under threat!

During the second session of rehearsal, 'Tina the Hooligan' returned with a vengeance.

As the afternoon light faded, technicians from Westair TV set up a sound and lighting system. Huge arc-lamps were suddenly switched on. Roving white spotlights changed to mood colours and swept the stage with a kaleidoscope of vivid reds, blues, and greens. It was all too much for Tina to bear.

When the loudspeakers were tested, Tina

went berserk. Her ears flattened against her head like a winged war helmet. Her eyes rolled and the teeth came out from beneath curled lips.

If you didn't know that Tina was really a gentle pussycat, you could easily have thought she was a wild, crazed, beast from hell.

'Is she acting?' asked Mr Coot nervously.

Danni tightened her grip on Tina's head collar and grimaced. Then Tina kicked out with her hind legs and sent a huge stage prop flying into space. Danni couldn't hold on. Tina was now free and running amok. She lunged at everything in sight, including a technician who was waving a light meter at her. Within minutes

she had destroyed almost every piece of scenery on the set. Then she started on the actors.

'Switch off the lights,' yelled Danni. 'And stop waving those swords at her!'

Danni managed to catch hold of Tina and led her away into a quiet corner to calm down.

Mr Coot sat in the middle of his ruined production, pulling at the last remaining strands of his hair, sobbing.

Tina was shaking from head to hoof. Samson sensed that something was wrong and nuzzled up against the fretting donkey.

Tina calmed down almost immediately as Samson licked her muzzle and blew up her nostrils. She stopped shaking and made funny, contented donkey noises in her throat. Then she pouted her mouth, which meant she wanted something to eat.

Lynne Gregory fed Tina a currant bun.

'It's amazing the effect that little blind donkey can have on others,' she exclaimed. 'I can see that it's not only children who benefit,' she added.

Mr Coot came marching over to read Danni the riot act. But it wasn't Danni's fault, as Jenny explained when she stepped in, before the director could open his mouth to speak.

'We should never have agreed to let you use one of our donkeys in the first place,' argued Jenny. 'They're not trained for this kind of work. You should have gone to the animal actors' agency and paid the proper fee for a professional performer.'

You tell him, Mum! Danni thought this to herself. She didn't say anything though. She would give her mum a hug for it later.

Mr Coot was speechless. He thought for a moment, looking as though he was about to explode. Then he took a few deep breaths and spoke calmly.

'The production is relying on your donkey,' he said. 'Particularly in the final scene. The television company have the programme slot booked and advertised as a "live" performance. Considering that your donkey has just destroyed all the scenery, I think there should be no

73

question about the donkey fulfilling its contract for tomorrow's performance.'

It was true what Mr Coot said. Tina had ruined everything. And without Tina there would be no performance. Viewers of Westair TV would be watching blank screens for an hour and a half instead of the advertised play. And Jenny felt that it was all her fault for allowing it to happen in the first place.

Suddenly, Lynne Gregory had an idea. While everything had been utter pandemonium, she had noticed that Samson had remained quite unmoved. Whilst everyone was rushing around screaming and shouting; while spotlights blazed and loud speakers blared, the little blind donkey had stayed very calm.

'Samson would be perfect for the role,' she noted. 'Nothing seems to upset him!'

Lynne Gregory was absolutely right. All those years of pulling Skinner's scrap-cart through the streets had made Samson used to loud noises and shouting. And being blind, the lights and action scenes didn't bother him one bit. As long as he had someone he trusted nearby, Samson would be perfect.

It seemed the only solution. Jenny agreed to let Samson stand in for Tina for the rest of the rehearsal. But only on a trial basis. She definitely wasn't going to risk any further distress to *any* Sanctuary donkey. At the first sign of anxiety, they were all going home.

The Roman fortress—one hour later

It went like clockwork. The entire cast and crew gave Samson a round of applause as he calmly crossed the stage in the final scene. Danni was so proud of him. She felt a bucketful of tears welling in her eyes. Samson, it appeared, was a true star performer.

Mr Coot had a sudden change of heart about the scenery too. He decided that the natural surroundings of the Roman fortress looked much better without the artificial props. They would use the mood lights to create their own,

natural scenery. It would be brilliant. He had Tina to thank for that brainwave. Hooligans have their uses too!

Everything was perfect. The rehearsed production promised to be a great success. And everybody was looking forward to Saturday evening. The weather forecast was excellent. Surely nothing could go wrong. Could it?

The Roman fortress—Saturday evening

The wide expanse of tiered steps at the rear of the fortress provided ideal seating for the excited audience.

Everyone from Tarbrooke seemed to be there. Old Mr Skinner had even persuaded the hospital doctors to let him attend. He was sitting with a nurse and looking forward to seeing Samson perform. The television crew had set up all their equipment. Lights and sound checks had been completed. The actors were in costume and the stage was set.

Danni held Samson by his head collar and glanced up at the sky. There wasn't a cloud in sight. The evening sun turned the stone fortress to gold. The silence was almost deafening. A few hushed whispers from the crowd floated down to the stage. A distant gull rose on a current of warm air and called like an echo across the scene.

Danni scanned the audience. She could see her parents, Kristie, and Tim seated in the front row. Tim gave her the thumbs up. Danni saw Lynne Gregory with Toby sitting just behind. Her stomach churned with butterflies as she recognized all the familiar faces.

The television cameras rolled into position.

Then, with only ten minutes to go before the 'live' performance of the *The Further Adventures of Don Quixote* was on air . . . it happened. Disaster struck. The child who was playing the young prince in the final scene fainted. Apparently, he hadn't been feeling well all day. And now he was being sick behind a pillar and definitely not up to the part.

Mr Coot wasn't amused. Mr Coot was about to burst into flames. Then Danni had an idea. Although it was an important part of the play, it was only a small role. No more than a simple ride across the stage. It required a small child of about seven. Toby would be perfect.

Mr Coot wasn't sure. But Mr Coot didn't have much choice. With five minutes to airtime, Toby was dressed in his costume and standing in the wings with his mother, waiting for his ride across the stage on Samson. Toby was very excited. But he was watching Samson and remained calm.

Lights . . . Cameras . . . Action!!

Westair Television presents *The Further Adventures of Don Quixote*. The cameras rolled.

As if by clockwork, the production went into autodrive. The well-rehearsed actors delivered their lines and acted their socks off.

Danni led Samson on and off the set as the role required, and the little blind donkey behaved perfectly. Danni tried not to look at the camera but couldn't wait to get home and watch the video. She felt like a movie star. It was ace!

The fading sun provided a spectacular sunset for the final scene. And everyone held

their breath as little Toby rode Samson across the stage.

The applause filled the fortress as the credits were scrolled onto film. It had been a fantastic success. And for many, Samson had been the star of the show.

The Sanctuary, late that evening

Danni couldn't wait until the morning. She wanted to watch the video of the play as soon as she got home. Like right now!

And it was brill! Everything looked different on the television screen. The setting looked smaller, but just as fantastic. The action and drama seemed more intense. The colours and costumes were brilliantly vibrant. And Samson looked absolutely incredible. His silver-grey coat shone like satin under the spotlights. And the final scene where he carried Toby across the stage was awesome.

The setting sun glowed orange behind them,

and there was this huge close-up of Danni. At one point her face filled the entire screen. Danni said it was gross. But secretly she liked it, even though she noticed a huge spot on her forehead. Tim joked and said the close-up was scary. Jenny and Peter thought it was beautiful.

Toby looked so proud as he sat tall in Samson's saddle. And when the credits scrolled at the end of the play, there was a special 'thanks' to The Sanctuary for allowing one of their 'residents' to perform in the production. That was a surprise. It had been Mr Coot's idea.

The Sanctuary—Monday morning

It was a morning like any other morning at the donkey sanctuary. The 'residents' had been checked, fed, and cuddled. Now they were grazing or dozing peacefully in the paddocks and surrounding fields.

Tina was stuck like glue to Samson and acting like his number one fan. Then the telephone rang. It was the animal actors' agency offering Samson starring roles in forthcoming productions on stage, film, and TV.

Jenny smiled to herself and said, 'Thank you, but, no!' Samson had a much more important role to play at The Sanctuary. Jenny was meeting with Lynne Gregory later, to discuss plans for the 'special needs' riding classes she was starting. There were lots of children like Toby who would benefit from donkey magic. And Jenny couldn't wait to get started.

She thought her donkeys were the most beautiful little animals in the world. And she was right.

Other books in the series

Donkey Danger

ISBN 0 19 275122 0

Danni's parents run a donkey sanctuary at their home on Whistlewind Farm and there's nothing Danni and her friend, Tim, enjoy more than helping to look after all the donkeys. But the sanctuary is short of funds so Danni decides to do a sponsored point-to-point with Shadow, her racing donkey.

As they journey around the local countryside Danni meets several people who tell her about a new donkey retirement home. But there's something about their stories that worries Danni. Who is the strange man who is buying up all the local donkeys? And where exactly is this mystery retirement home?

Donkey Disaster

ISBN 0 19 275123 9

The donkey sanctuary at Whistlewind Farm has started a bed and breakfast service to raise some funds. The first guests at the Farm are Robyn Springer and her mother. Robyn loves the farm and spends all her time helping out with the donkeys, but unfortunately her mother is not so keen on getting herself mucky!

But when Mrs Springer learns about a plan to build a factory in the field next to the sanctuary, she is determined to do all she can to keep the donkeys safe and the field free from development.

Other Oxford books

The Tales of Olga da Polga
Michael Bond

ISBN 0 19 275130 1

From the very beginning there was not the slightest doubt that Olga da Polga was the sort of guinea-pig who would go places.

Olga da Polga is no ordinary guinea-pig. From the rosettes in her fur to her unusual name, there's something special about her ... and Olga knows it!

Olga has a wild imagination, and from the minute she arrives at her new home, she begins entertaining all the other animals in the garden with her outrageous tales and stories – but she still has time to get up to all kinds of mischief and have lots of wonderful adventures too.

Olga Meets Her Match

Michael Bond

ISBN 0 19 275132 8

Just in front of her there was an opening in the wall of the main building which she hadn't noticed before, and standing barely a whisker's length away in the darkness beyond was another guinea-pig . For a moment neither of them spoke, and then the other stirred.

'You must be Olga,' he said. 'I was told you were coming.'

Olga da Polga goes visiting and meets Boris, a Russian guinea-pig. Olga and Boris become firm friends and Olga is surprised to discover that Boris can tell even taller tales than she can! Soon the time comes for her to return to her own garden, but Olga doesn't mind, she can't wait to tell the other animals all about her trip and, of course, her new friend, and she even gives them all a demonstration of her Russian dancing skills . . .

Olga Moves House

Michael Bond

ISBN 0 19 275129 8

No one in the Sawdust family could remember exactly when it happened, but happen it did. One moment Olga was living in her hutch in the garden, the next moment she had moved into their house. Once there, she made herself very much at home in a corner of the dining room; as large as life 'thank you very much', and often – especially when it was getting near meal times – twice as noisy.

Winter has come to the Sawdust household, and Olga's been moved into a new home, inside the house. She's very excited about her new home and has even managed to get Mrs Sawdust to do a spot of redecorating! Olga enjoys watching the comings and goings inside the house and still manages to get herself into mischief whilst embarking on many wonderful adventures.

Simone's Letters

Helena Pielichaty

ISBN 0 19 275087 9

Dear Mr Cakebread . . . For starters my name is Simone, not Simon . . . Mum says you sound just like my dad. My dad, Dennis, lives in Bartock with his girlfriend, Alexis . . . My mum says lots of rude things about her because Alexis was one of the reasons my parents got divorced (I was the other) . . .

When ten-year-old Simone starts writing letters to Jem Cakebread, the leading man of a touring theatre company, she begins a friendship that will change her life . . . and the lives of all around her: her mum, her best friend Chloe, her new friend Melanie – and not forgetting Jem himsellf.

This collection of funny and often touching letters charts Simone's final year at Primary School; from a school visit to *Rumpelstiltskin's Revenge* to her final leaving Assembly; through the ups and downs of her friendships – and those of her mum and dad.

Simone's Diary
Helena Pielichaty

ISBN 0 19 275136 0

Dear Mr Cohen . . . Hi, it's me, Simone Anna Wibberley. Do you remember me from when you were a student on teaching practice with Miss Cassidy's class? . . . I am applying to be in your experiment . . . I will answer everything as fully as I can . . . I am quite good at this sort of things because I used to fill in a lot of questionnaires in magazines with my dad's ex-girlfiend, Alexis . . .

Simone has left Woodhill Primary School behind her and is starting life at her new secondary school. It's a little bit scary and there are lots of new things to get used to, so when she's asked to start writing a journal about her new experiences at Bartock High School, it's the perfect opportunity for Simone to write down all her thoughts and ideas in her own inimitable style.